USBORNE

FIRST THOUSAND WORDS

STICKER BOOK

Heather Amery
Illustrated by Stephen Cartwright

Edited by Lisa Miles
Designed by Fiona Johnson

Hear the words on the internet

You can listen to all the words in this book on the Usborne Quicklinks Website. Just go to **www.usborne-quicklinks.com** and enter the keywords **1000 english**. There you can:

- listen to the first thousand words

- find links to other useful websites for language learners about the English language, Britain and the USA.

Note for parents and guardians

Please ensure that your children read and follow the internet safety guidelines displayed on the Usborne Quicklinks Website.

The links in Usborne Quicklinks are regularly reviewed and updated. However, the content of a website may change at any time, and Usborne Publishing is not responsible for the content on any website other than its own. We recommend that children are supervised while on the internet, that they do not use internet chat rooms and that you use internet filtering software to block unsuitable material. For more information, see the **Net Help** area on the Usborne Quicklinks Website.

On every double page with pictures, there is a little yellow duck to look for. Can you find it?

About this book

All young children will enjoy this entertaining picture sticker book. Parents and teachers sharing it with them will discover that each page provides lively situations to explore, and to talk and laugh about.

With this book, children can be introduced to the printed words, and, with help and encouragement, they can match the words to the word and picture stickers. The book can also be used as a picture word book for looking and talking.

The *First Thousand Words Sticker Book* is designed to be used at many different levels, so that children of various ages and abilities will find it stimulating and amusing.

There is a word list at the back of the book, which brings together all the words in alphabetical order. It can be used to encourage children to look up words and find the right page and picture. This is an important skill, which will prepare children to use simple information books and dictionaries.

About the stickers

Each grey box shows a word. Find the correct word and picture sticker to fit into each grey box. The stickers can be removed and used again if you don't get it right first time.

spacemen

frog   frog

cockerel

3

At home

bath

soap

tap

toilet paper

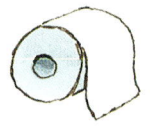

toothbrush

water

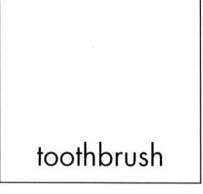

toilet

sponge

washbasin

bathroom

living room

shower

toothpaste

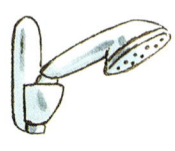

radio

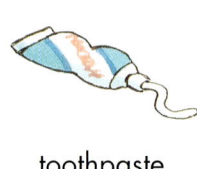

cushion

CD

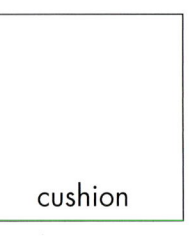

carpet

sofa

4

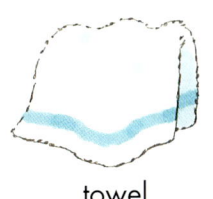 towel

chair

duvet

 comb

sheet

bed

 rug

bedroom

hall

wardrobe

pillow

 chest of drawers

mirror

brush

 lamp

pictures

pegs

radiator

video

newspaper

 table

letters

stairs

 telephone

5

The kitchen

fridge

glasses

clock

stool

teaspoons

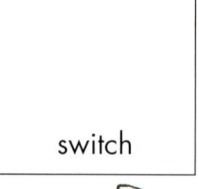
switch

washing powder

key

door

vacuum cleaner

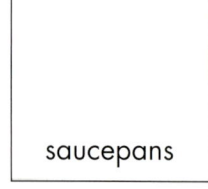
saucepans

forks

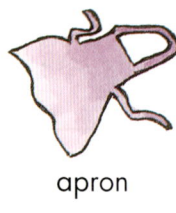
apron

ironing board

rubbish

tea towel

| sink | kettle 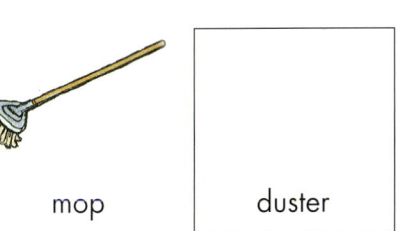 | knives | mop | duster | tiles  |

broom

washing machine

dustpan

drawer

saucers

frying pan

cooker

spoons

| cups | matches | brush | bowls | cupboard | iron | plates  |

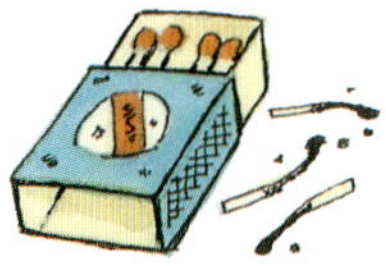

wheelbarrow

beehive	
snail	

bricks

pigeon	
spade	

ladybird

dustbin	
seeds	

shed

The garden

worm	flowers	sprinkler	hoe	wasp	grass

8

watering can

bee

trowel

bone

hedge

fork

lawn mower

path

leaves

tree

smoke

caterpillar

rake

pram

ladder

bonfire

hosepipe

greenhouse

sticks

bird's nest

9

vice

sandpaper

drill

ladder

saw

sawdust

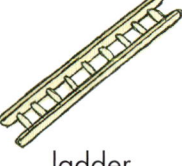

calendar

tool box

screwdriver

The workshop

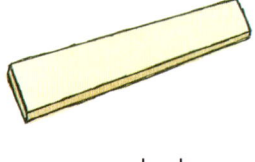

plank

shavings

penknife

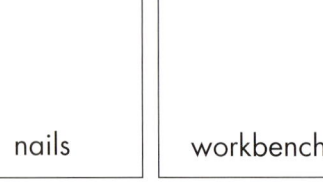

wood

nails

workbench

duster

10

screws

tacks	

spider

bolts

nuts

cobweb

barrel

fly

axe

cat | jars | plane | paint pot | file | hammer | tape measure

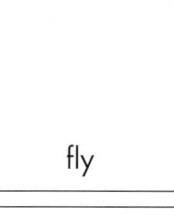

11

shop

hole

café

ambulance

pavement

aerial

chimney

roof

digger

The street

hotel

man

police car

pipes

drill

school

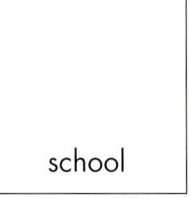
playground

12

| bus | taxi | crossing | factory | lorry | traffic lights |

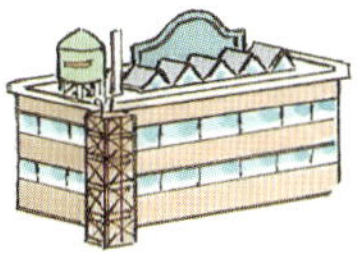

cinema

van

roller

trailer

house

market

steps

motorcycle

flats

| bicycle | fire engine | policeman | car | woman | lamp post |

13

train set

recorder

dice

robot

drums

necklace

camera

beads

dolls

The toyshop

guitar

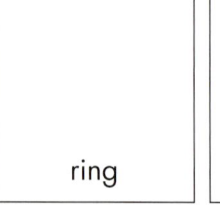
ring

doll's house

whistle

bricks

castle

submarine

14

 mouth organ

bow	parachute	 boat	face paints	roller

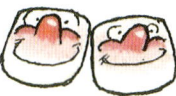 masks

 racing car

rocking horse

 money box

marbles

puppets

piano

spacemen

rocket

 trumpet

arrows	crane	 modelling dough	gun	soldiers

 paints

15

swings

The park

sandpit

picnic

kite

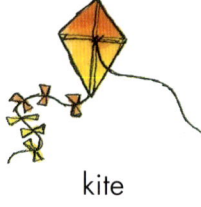

ice cream

dog

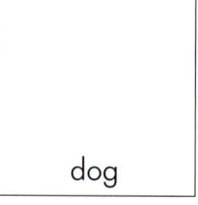

gate

path

frog

slide

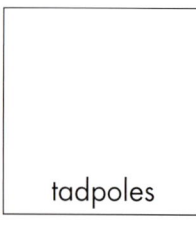

tadpoles

lake

roller blades

bush

flower bed

swans

bench

baby

skateboard

earth

push-chair

seesaw

children

tricycle

birds

railings

ball

yacht

lead

duck

trees

skipping rope

ducklings

puddle

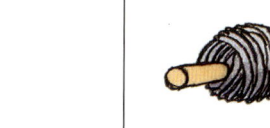

string

17

The zoo

panda

wing

eagle

hippopotamus

gorilla

paws

kangaroo

bat

monkey

tail

wolf

iceberg

penguin

crocodile

bear

pelican

feathers

ostrich

dolphin

giraffe

lion

cubs

18

horns

deer

camel

seal

tortoise

polar bear

trunk

bison

elephant

rhinoceros

snake

goat

zebra

beaver

shark

whale

tiger

leopard

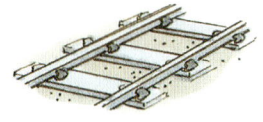

railway track

Travel

engine

buffers

carriages

train driver

goods train

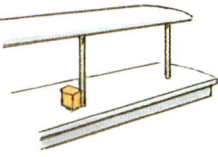

platform

ticket inspector

suitcase

ticket machine

The railway station

The garage

signals

backpack

headlights

engine

wheel

battery

The airport

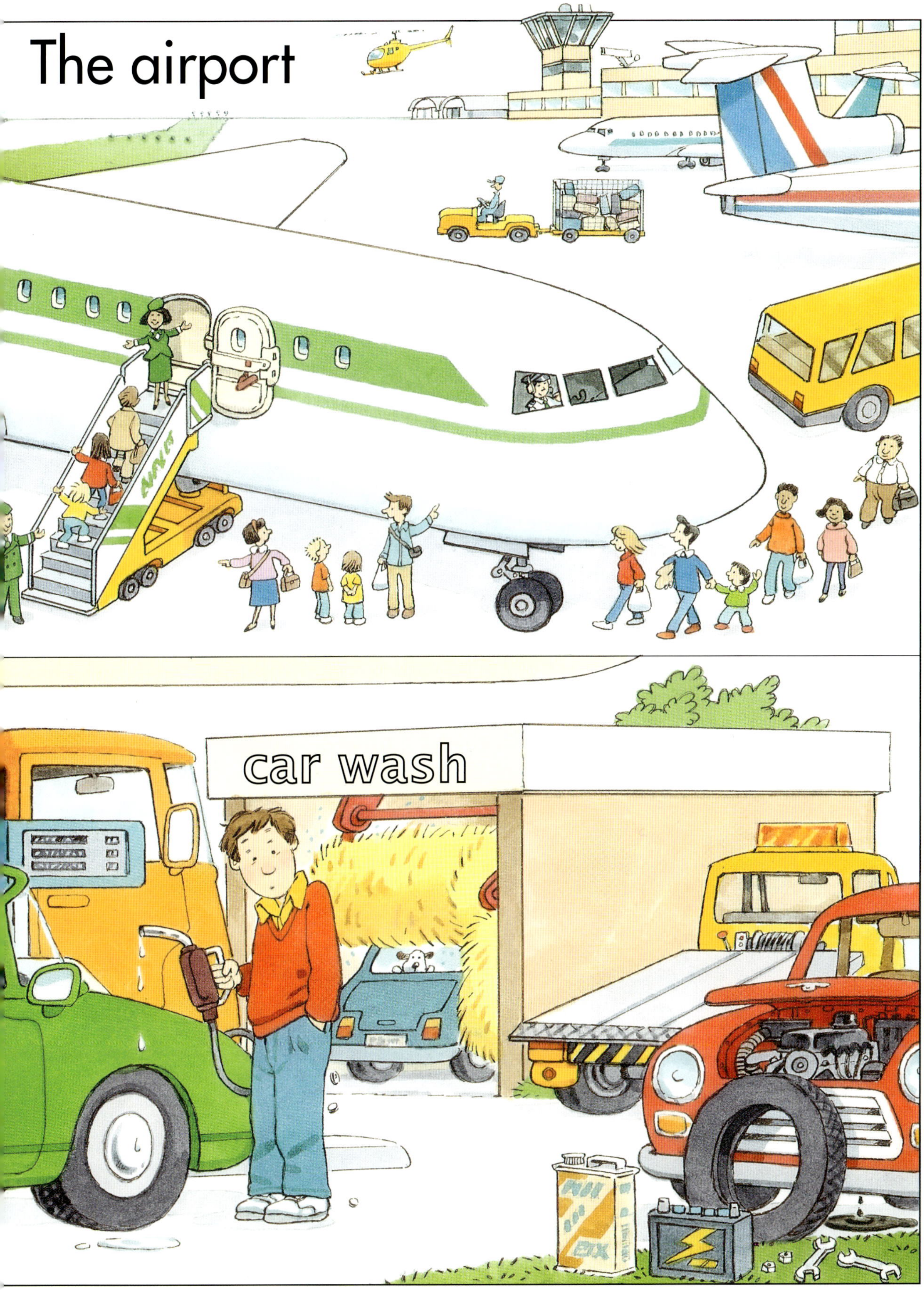

air hostess

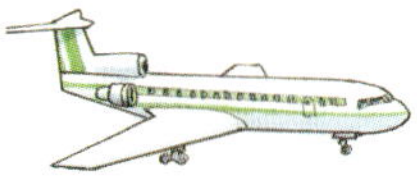

runway

air steward

control tower

pilot

car wash

boot

petrol

car wash

petrol tanker

spanner

tyre

bonnet

oil

petrol pump

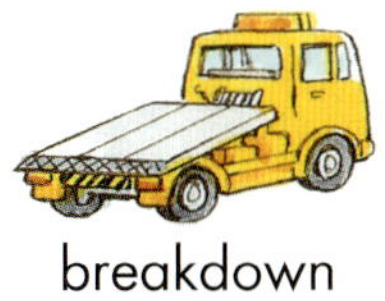

breakdown lorry

21

windmill

The country

hot-air balloon

butterfly

lizard

stones

fox

stream

signpost

hedgehog

lock

squirrel

forest

badger

river

road

rocks

mountain

tents

canal

logs

village

moth

bridge

barge

waterfall

owl

tunnel

toad

train

caravan

hill

fisherman

mole

fox cubs

haystack

sheepdog

ducks

lambs

pond

chicks

loft

pigsty

bull

ducklings

The farm

cockerel

hen house

tractor

geese

tanker

barn

mud

| farmer |  field |  hens | calf | fence | saddle |  cowshed |

 cow

plough

orchard

stable

piglets

shepherdess

turkeys

scarecrow

|  cart | hay | sheep |  straw bales | horse | pigs |  farmhouse |

25

The seaside

sailing boat

sea

oar

lighthouse

spade

bucket

starfish

sandcastle

umbrella

flag

sailor

crab

seagull

island

motor-boat   water-skier

| shell | waves | sunhat | cliff  | ship |

ship

canoe

rope

pebbles

seaweed

net

paddle

fishing boat

flippers

| swimsuit | oil tanker | beach | rowing boat | deck chair | fish | donkey |

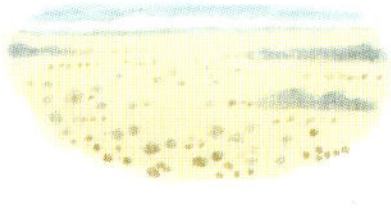

scissors

sums

rubber

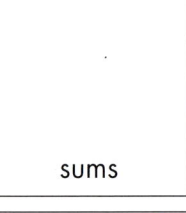

ruler

photographs

felt-tips

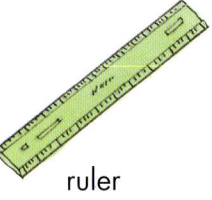

drawing pins

paints

boy

At school

 pencil

desk

books

 pen

glue

chalk

 drawing

wastepaper bin

board

teacher

box

map

brush

ceiling

wall

floor

notebook

alphabet

badge

aquarium

paper

blind

a b c d e f g
h i j k l m n
o p q r s t u
v w x y z

door handle

plant

globe

girl

crayons

lamp

easel

29

nurse

The hospital

apple

syringe

cotton wool

medicine

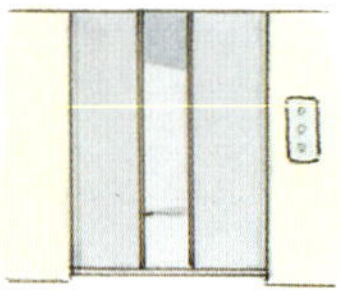

lift

dressing gown

crutches

pills

tray

watch

thermometer

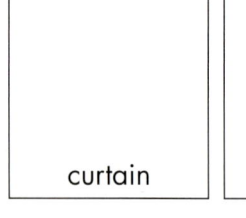

curtain

plaster

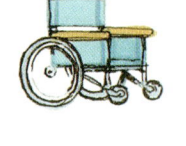

wheelchair

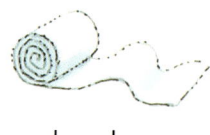

bandage

jigsaw

doctor

The doctor

teddy bear	slippers	computer

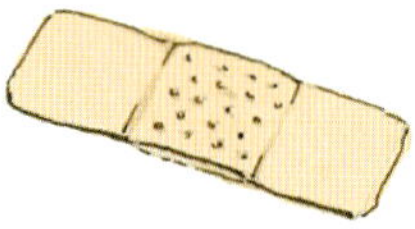

sticking plaster

banana

grapes

basket

toys

pear

cards

nappy

walking stick

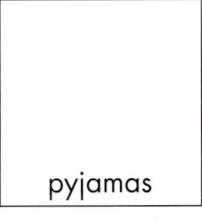
television

nightdress

pyjamas

orange

tissues

comic

waiting room

31

balloon

chocolate

sweet

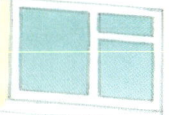

window

fireworks

ribbon

cake

straw

candle

The party

paper chain

toys

sandwich

butter

biscuit

cheese

beaker

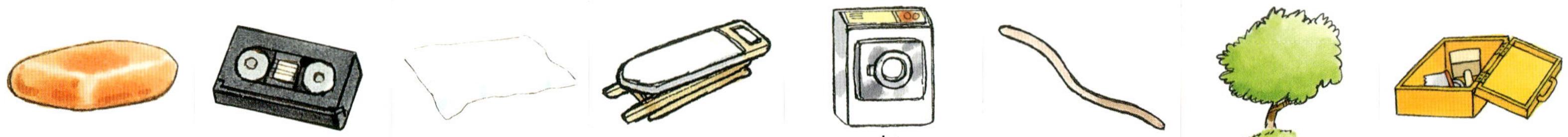

soap	video	sheet	ironing board	washing machine
worm	tree	tool box		

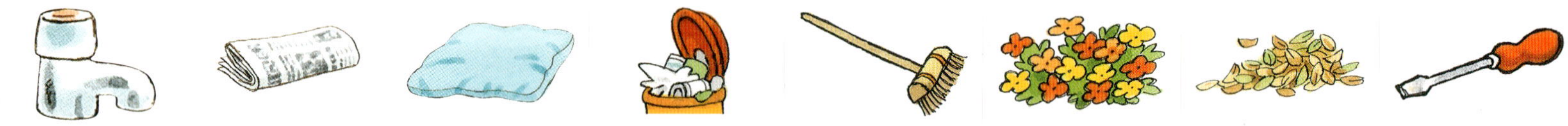

tap	newspaper	duvet	rubbish	broom
flowers	leaves	screwdriver		

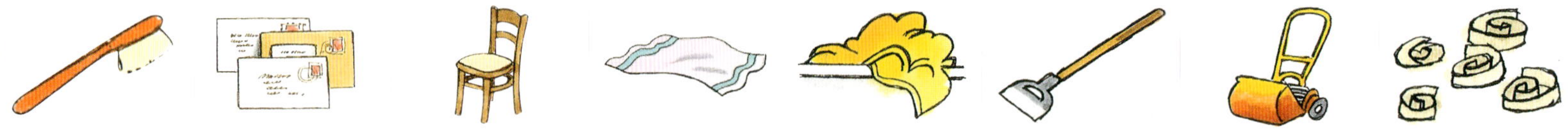

toothbrush	letters	chair	tea towel	duster
hoe	lawn mower	shavings		

water	stairs	glasses	cups	knives
wasp	fork	penknife		

sponge	pegs	clock	brush	sink
grass	bone	nails		

washbasin	pictures	teaspoons	bowls	beehive
pram	bee	workbench		

radio	brush	switch	iron	snail
ladder	watering can	jars		

cushion	mirror	key	spoons	pigeon
hosepipe	sandpaper	plane		

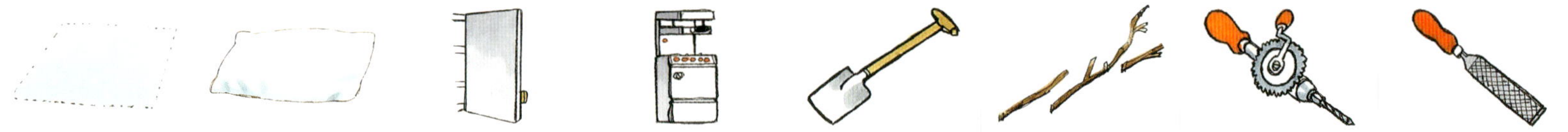

carpet	pillow	door	cooker	spade
sticks	drill	file		

sofa	wardrobe	saucepans	saucers	dustbin
rake	saw	hammer		

radiator	bed	forks	drawer	seeds
caterpillar	sawdust	axe		

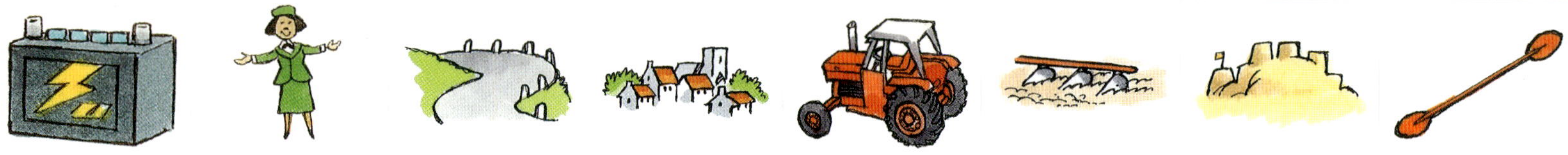

battery | air hostess | road | village | tractor | plough | sandcastle | paddle

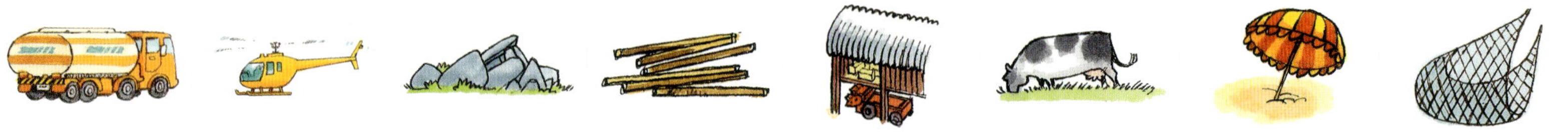

petrol tanker | helicopter | rocks | logs | barn | cow | umbrella | net

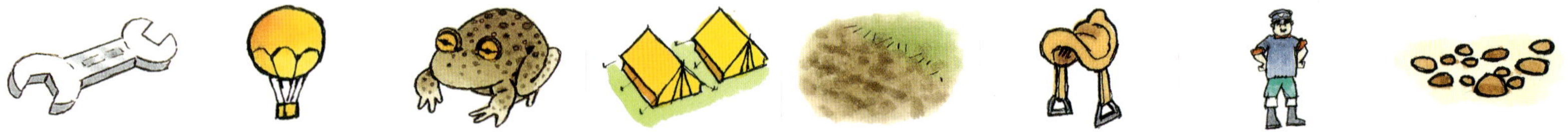

spanner | hot-air balloon | toad | tents | mud | saddle | sailor | pebbles

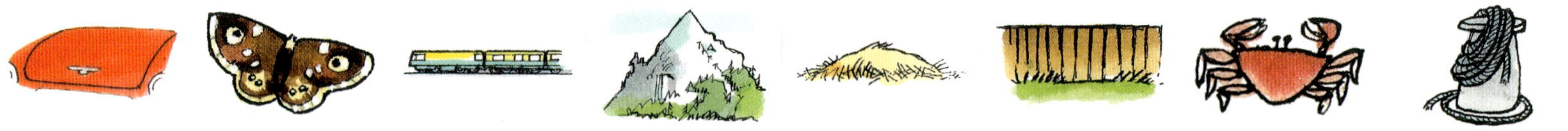

bonnet | butterfly | train | mountain | hay | fence | crab | rope

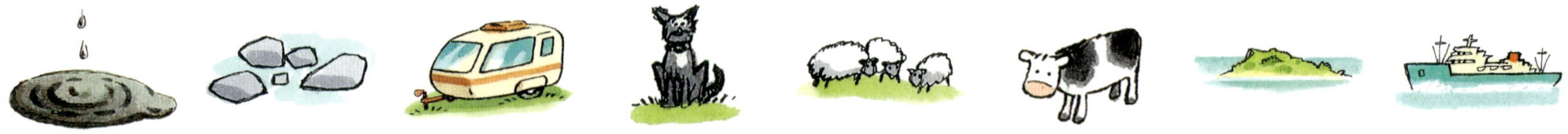

oil | stones | caravan | sheepdog | sheep | calf | island | ship

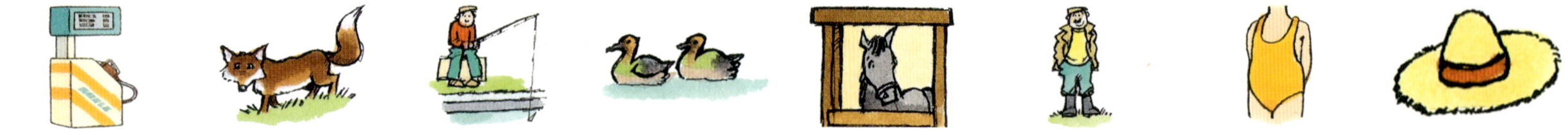

petrol pump | fox | fisherman | ducks | horse | farmer | swimsuit | sunhat

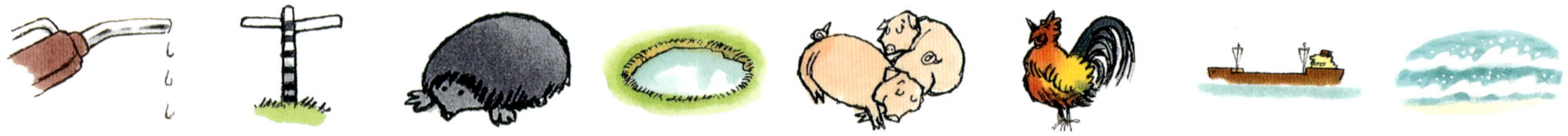

petrol | signpost | mole | pond | pigs | cockerel | oil tanker | waves

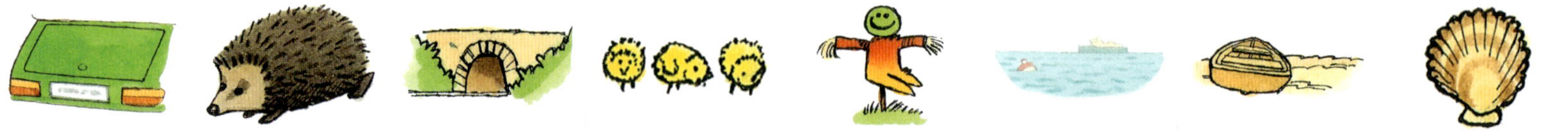

boot | hedgehog | tunnel | chicks | scarecrow | sea | rowing boat | shell

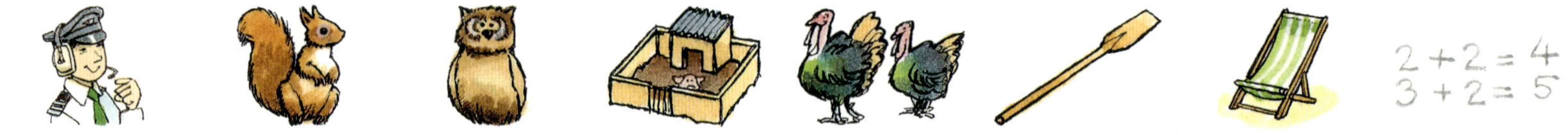

pilot | squirrel | owl | pigsty | turkeys | oar | deck chair | sums

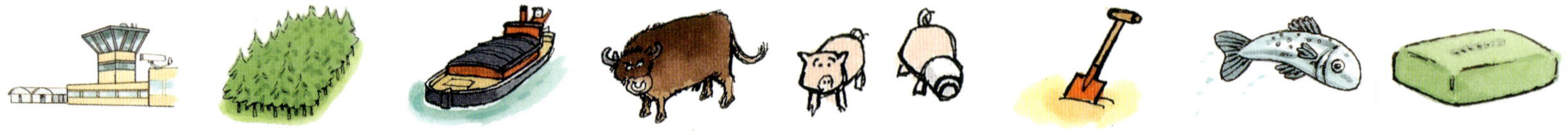

control tower | forest | barge | bull | piglets | spade | fish | rubber

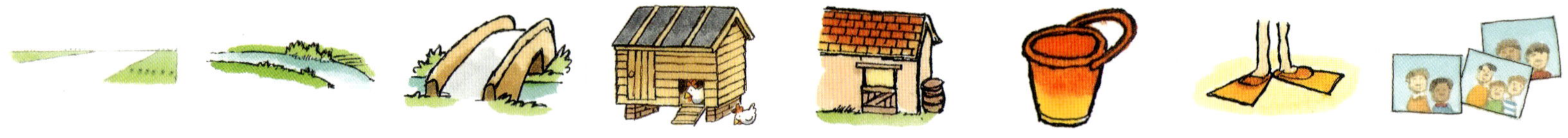

runway | river | bridge | hen house | stable | bucket | flippers | photographs

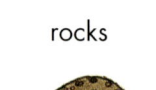

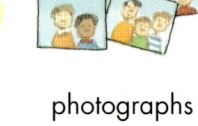

wing eagle	tiger	soup	back	sandals	fireman	smile	write
bat	milk	sauce	hand	gloves	dentist	cut	fight
pelican	sugar	mashed potatoes	fingers	belt	baker	make	wash
dolphin	hot chocolate	chopsticks	socks	zip	hairdresser	jump	pick
cubs	boiled egg	eyebrow	vest	buttons	painter	carry	fall
tortoise	rolls	mouth	jeans	coat	chef	skip	walk
goat	salt	teeth	shirt	cap	think	sleep	run
snake	pepper	chin	sweatshirt	trainers	catch	cook	high
seal	honey	neck	dress	butcher	break	read	low
beaver	chips	shorts	scarf	judge	crawl	watch	under

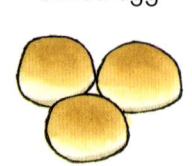

fat

cold

photographer

rabbit

diving

white

cone

dodgems

thin

hot

tourists

food

archery

black

circle

trick cyclist

big

small

alive

Christmas tree

mouse

target

grey

square

trapeze

empty

dead

lightning

goldfish

jogging

red

popcorn

rabbit

top hat

full

old

wind

snowboarding

badminton

pink

hoop-la

circus dog

hard

new

frost

sailing

pony

oval

one

soft

front

dew

gym

table tennis

three

five

seven

dark

back

guinea pig

dance

nine

eleven

bride

light

bridegroom

thirteen

fifteen

first

seventeen

last

plane

nineteen

felt-tips
blind
medicine
tissues
chocolate
video camera
cucumber
trolley
paints
paper
dressing gown
comic
sweet
raspberry
celery
money
boy
badge
crutches
walking stick
fireworks
fruit juice
apricot
purse
desk
abcdefg
hijklmno
pqrstu
vwxyx
alphabet
tray
nappy
ribbon
cherry
onion
bottles
books
floor
watch
pear
straw
crisps
cabbage
basket
glue
wall
curtain
toys
candle
sausage
lettuce
pineapple
chalk
brush
plaster
grapes
toys
salami
peas
meat
plant
map
jigsaw
banana
sandwich
clementine
tomato
scales
girl
teacher
doctor
computer
biscuit
carrot
spinach
flour
crayons
board
syringe
slippers
cheese
cauliflower
beans
eggs
lamp
cotton wool
pyjamas
teddy bear
tablecloth
mushroom
pumpkin
carrier bag

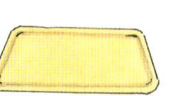

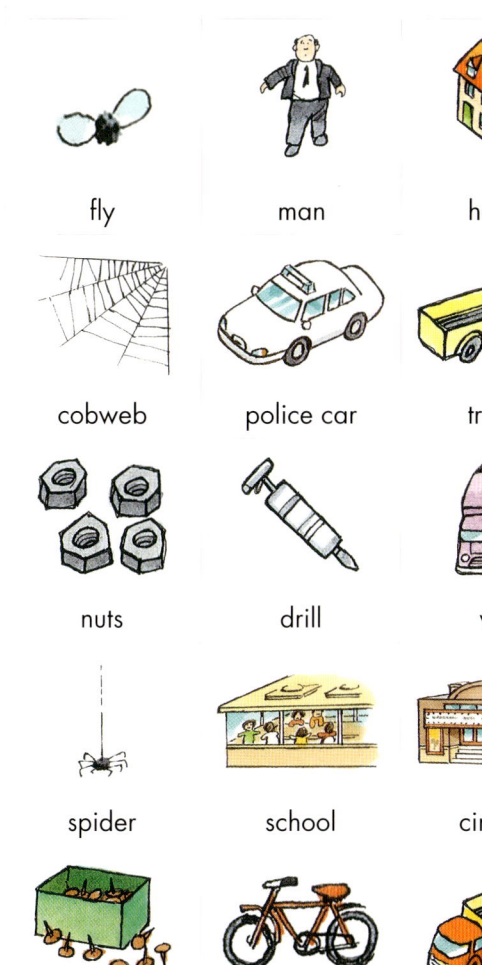 fly	man	house	necklace	soldiers	sandpit	duck	baby
cobweb	police car	trailer	beads	rocket	picnic	trees	engine
nuts	drill	van	dolls	spacemen	ice cream	ducklings	buffers
spider	school	cinema	ring	puppets	dog	puddle	trail driver
tracks	bicycle	lorry	doll's house	marbles	path	yacht	goods train
hole	fire engine	crossing	bricks	rocking horse	frog	ball	ticket inspector
café	policeman	taxi	castle	racing car	tadpoles	birds	suitcase
pavement	woman	bus	submarine	roller	lake	tricycle	signals
aerial	lamp post	recorder	arrows	face paints	bush	seesaw	backpack
roof	motorcycle	dice	crane	parachute	flower bed	push-chair	headlights
digger	steps	drums	gun	bow	swans	skateboard	wheel

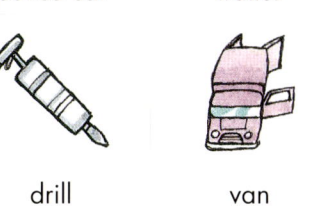

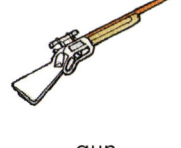

presents

clementine

salami

cassette tape

sausage

crisps

fancy dress

cherry

raspberry

jack-in-the-box

video camera

bread

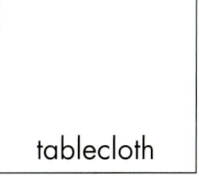

tablecloth

bulb

fruit juice

strawberry

33

grapefruit

carrot

cauliflower

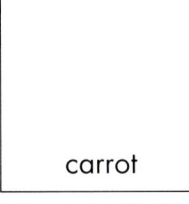

leek

mushroom

cucumber

lemon

celery

apricot

The shop

cheese

fruit and vegetables

melon

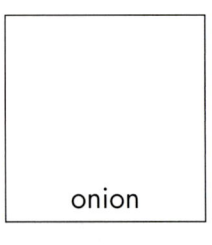

onion

cabbage

peach

lettuce

peas

tomato

carrier bag	eggs	plum	flour	scales

jars

meat

pineapple

yoghurt

basket

bottles

handbag

purse

money

potatoes	spinach	beans	checkout	pumpkin	trolley

tins

Food

breakfast

lunch or dinner

coffee

fried egg

toast

jam

cream

boiled egg

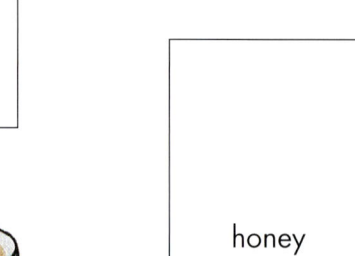
cereal

hot chocolate

milk

sugar

honey

salt

pepper

teapot

tea

pancakes

rolls

36

supper or tea

ham

soup

omelette

chopsticks

salad

hamburger

chicken

rice

sauce

spaghetti

mashed potatoes

pizza

chips

pudding

Me

head

hair

face

arm

elbow

tummy

toes

foot

leg

knee

eyebrow

eye

nose

cheek

mouth

lips

teeth

tongue

chin

ears

neck

shoulders

chest

back

bottom

hand

thumb

fingers

My clothes

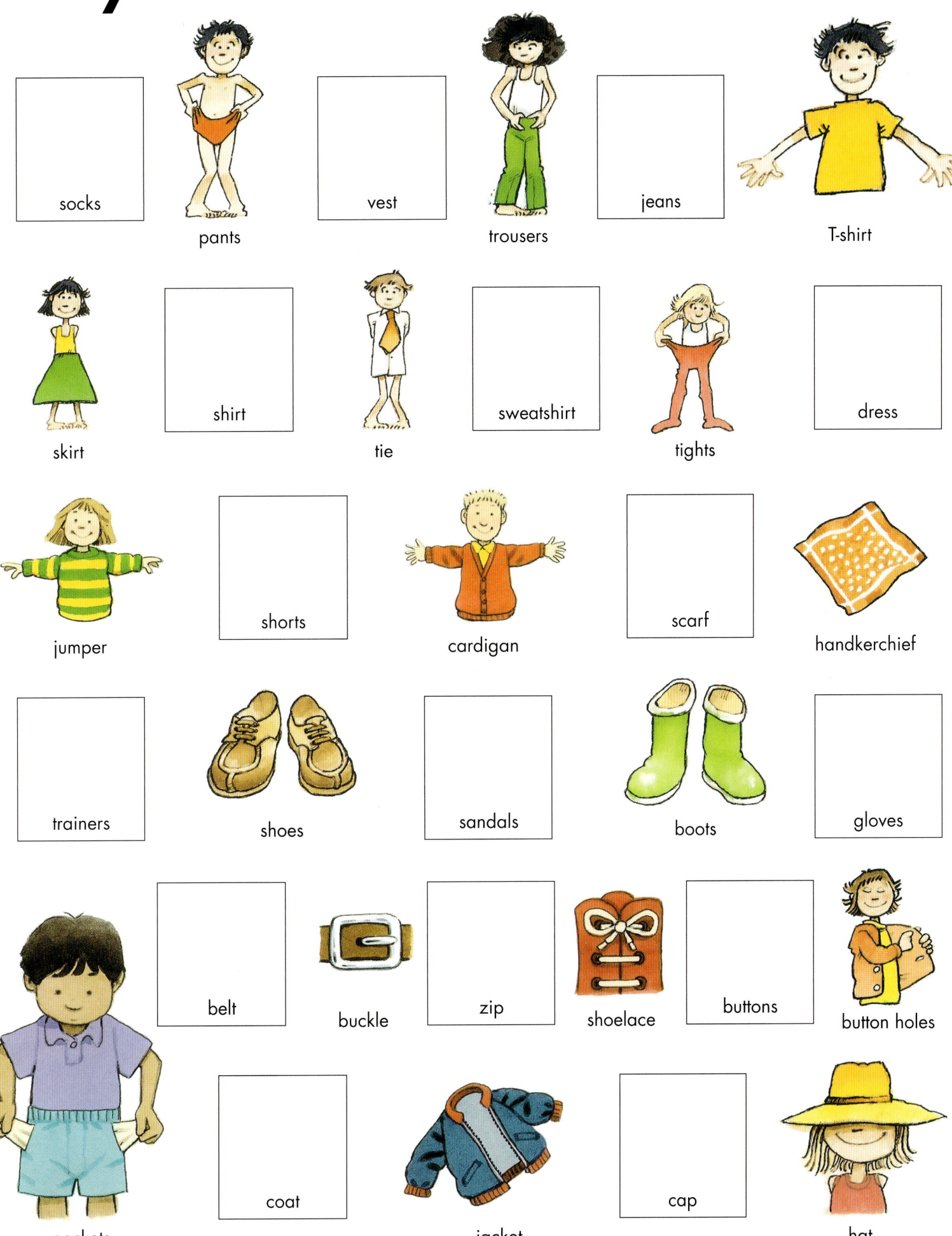

socks

pants

vest

trousers

jeans

T-shirt

skirt

shirt

tie

sweatshirt

tights

dress

jumper

shorts

cardigan

scarf

handkerchief

trainers

shoes

sandals

boots

gloves

belt

buckle

zip

shoelace

buttons

button holes

pockets

coat

jacket

cap

hat

39

People

actor   actress

chef

dancers

singer

singers

astronaut

butcher

policeman

policewoman

carpenter

fireman

artist

judge

mechanics

40

lorry driver

bus driver

dentist

waiter   waitress

postman

painter

frogman

baker

Families

grandfather

aunt   uncle

son
brother

daughter
sister

mother
wife

father
husband

pet

cousin

grandmother

41

Doing things

smile

cry

think

listen

laugh

catch

throw

break

paint

write

chop

cut

eat

talk

carry

dig

drink

jump

wash

knit

make

dance

42

play

crawl

watch

climb

take

skip

fight

sleep

sew

wait

cook

hide

read

buy

push

sing

blow

pull

sweep

pick

fall

walk

run

sit

43

Opposite words

good

bad

far

near

over

under

wet

dry

top

bottom

dirty

clean

low

high

closed

open

fat

thin

big

small

few

many

first

last

left

right

44

out

in

easy

difficult

front

back

empty

full

soft

hard

fast

slow

long

short

dark

light

cold

hot

new

old

dead

alive

upstairs

downstairs

45

Days

calendar

Monday
Tuesday
Wednesday
Thursday
Friday
Saturday
Sunday

morning

evening

sun

night

space

moon

star

planet

spaceship

telescope

Special days

birthday

birthday card

candle

present

birthday cake

holiday

tourists

plane

wedding day

bride

bridegroom

camera

photographer

Christmas day

Christmas tree

reindeer

Father Christmas

sleigh

Weather

umbrella

rain

lightning

fog

sun

clouds

sky

snow

dew

wind

mist

frost

rainbow

Seasons

spring

summer

autumn

winter

48

Pets

hamster

vet

kennel

guinea pig

puppy

dog

budgerigar

parrot

beak

rabbit

food

mouse

cage

canary

cat

basket

goldfish

kitten

milk

Sport and exercise

basketball

rowing

snowboarding

windsurfing

sailing

cricket

karate

racket

tennis

American football

gym

dance

ball

bat

baseball

fishing rod

fishing

bait

rugby

diving

swimming pool

swimming

race

50

archery

target

jogging

hang-gliding

helmet

badminton

judo

cycling

climbing

horse

locker

pony

changing room

riding

football

table tennis

ice skates

ice-skating

ski pole

chairlift

skis

sumo wrestling

skiing

51

Colours

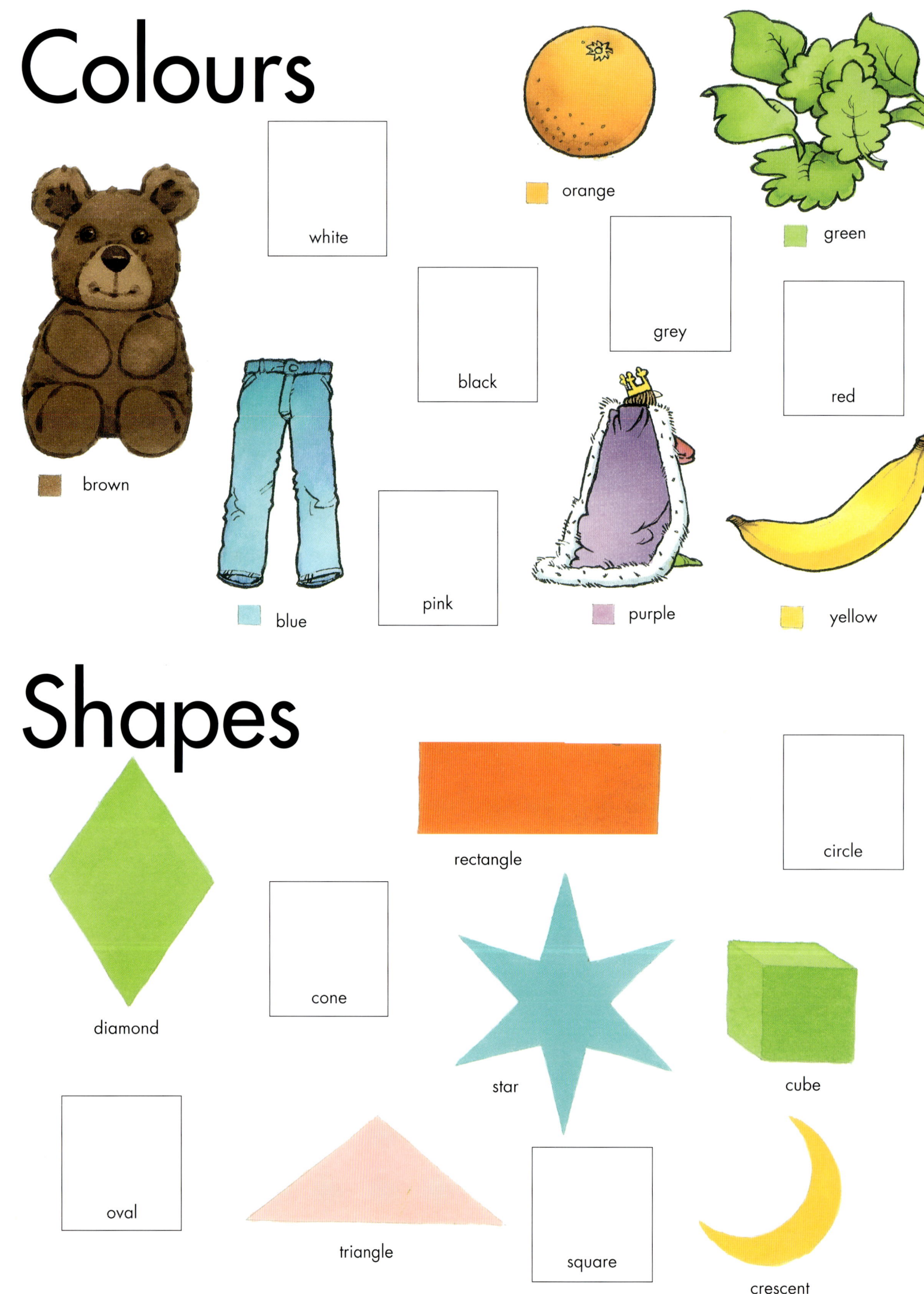

orange

green

white

grey

red

black

brown

blue

pink

purple

yellow

Shapes

rectangle

circle

diamond

cone

star

cube

oval

triangle

square

crescent

52

Numbers

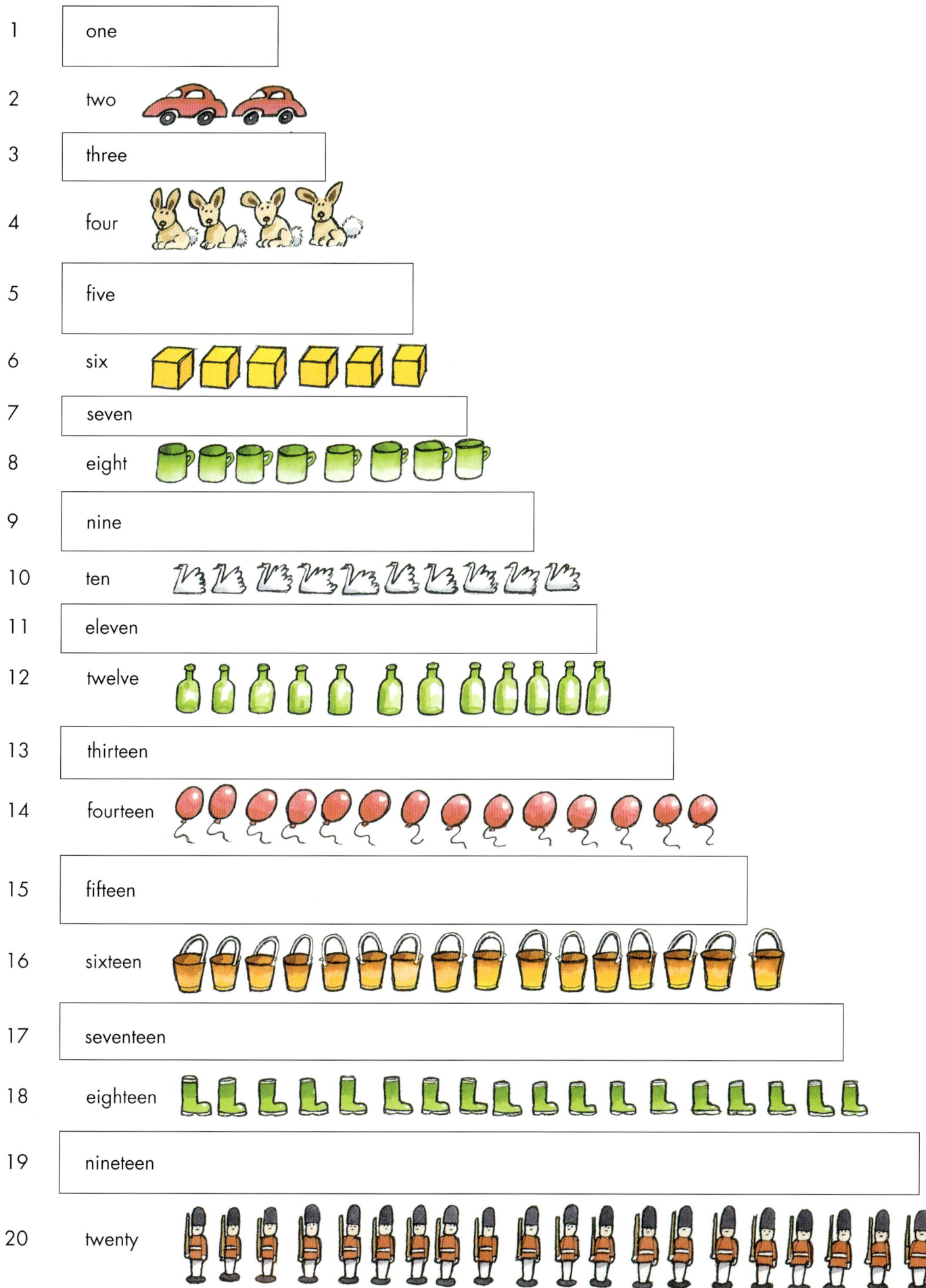

1	one	
2	two	
3	three	
4	four	
5	five	
6	six	
7	seven	
8	eight	
9	nine	
10	ten	
11	eleven	
12	twelve	
13	thirteen	
14	fourteen	
15	fifteen	
16	sixteen	
17	seventeen	
18	eighteen	
19	nineteen	
20	twenty	

The fairground

roundabout

mat

helter-skelter

big wheel

hoop-la

ghost train

popcorn

big dipper

dodgems

rifle range

candy floss

54

The circus

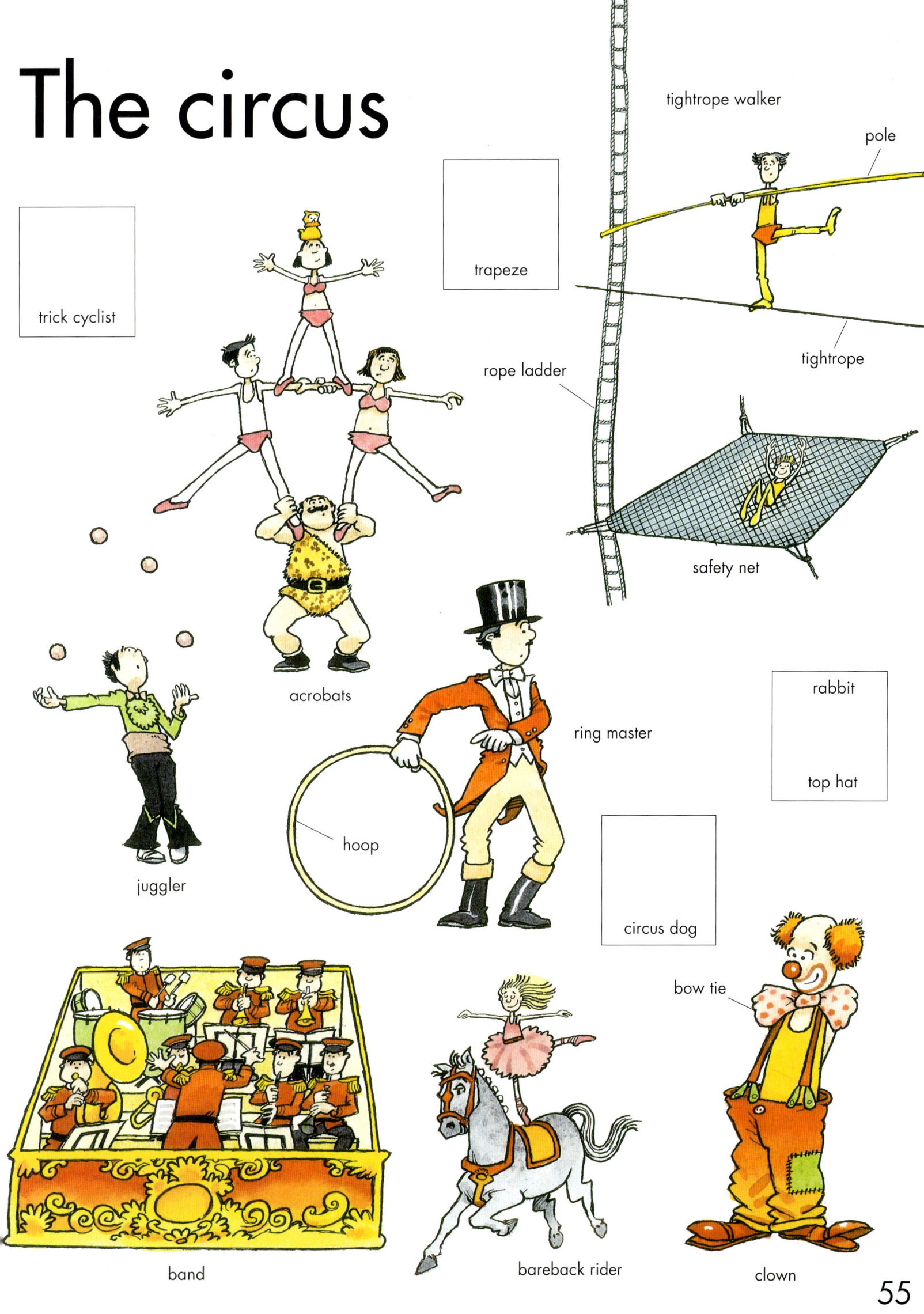

trick cyclist

trapeze

tightrope walker

pole

rope ladder

tightrope

safety net

acrobats

ring master

rabbit

top hat

hoop

juggler

circus dog

bow tie

band

bareback rider

clown

55

Words in order

This is a list of all the words in the pictures. They are in the same order as the alphabet. After each word is a number. This is a page number. On that page, you will find the word and a picture.

a

acrobats, 55
actor, 40
actress, 40
aerial, 12
air hostess, 21
airport, 21
air steward, 21
alive, 45
alphabet, 29
ambulance, 12
American football, 50
apple, 30
apricot, 34
apron, 6
aquarium, 29
archery, 51
arm, 38
arrows, 15
artist, 40
astronaut, 40
aunt, 41
autumn, 48
axe, 11

b

baby, 17
back (of body), 38
back (not front), 45
backpack, 20
bad, 44
badge, 29
badger, 22
badminton, 51

bait, 50
baker, 41
ball, 17, 50
balloon, 32
banana, 31
band, 55
bandage, 30
bareback rider, 55
barge, 23
barn, 24
barrel, 11
baseball, 50
basket, 31, 35, 49
basketball, 50
bat (animal), 18
bat (for sport), 50
bath, 4
bathroom, 4
battery, 20
beach, 27
beads, 14
beak, 49
beaker, 32
beans, 35
bear, 18, 19, 30
beaver, 19
bed, 5
bedroom, 5
bee, 9
beehive, 8
belt, 39
bench, 17
bicycle, 13
big, 44
big dipper, 54
big wheel, 54
birds, 17
bird's nest, 9
birthday, 47
birthday cake, 47
birthday card, 47
biscuit, 32
bison, 19
black, 52
blind (for a window), 29
blow, 43

blue, 52
board, 29
boat, 15, 26, 27
boiled egg, 36
bolts, 11
bone, 9
bonfire, 9
bonnet (of a car), 21
books, 28
boot (of a car), 21
boots, 39
bottles, 35
bottom (of body), 38
bottom (not top), 44
bow, 15
bowls, 7
bow tie, 55
box, 29
boy, 28
bread, 33
break, 42
breakdown lorry, 21
breakfast, 36
bricks, 8, 14
bride, 47
bridegroom, 47
bridge, 23
broom, 7
brother, 41
brown, 52
brush, 5, 7, 29
bucket, 26
buckle, 39
budgerigar, 49
buffers (train), 20
bulb (light), 33
bull, 24
bus, 13
bus driver, 41
bush, 16
butcher, 40
butter, 32
butterfly, 22
button holes, 39
buttons, 39
buy, 43

C

cabbage, 34
café, 12
cage, 49
cake, 32, 47
calendar, 10, 46
calf, 25
camel, 19
camera, 14, 47
canal, 23
canary, 49
candle, 32, 47
candy floss, 54
canoe, 27
cap, 39
car, 13
caravan, 23
cardigan, 39
cards, 31
carpenter, 40
carpet, 4
carriages, 20
carrier bag, 35
carrot, 34
carry, 42
cart, 25
car wash, 21
cassette tape, 33
castle, 14
cat, 11, 49
catch, 42
caterpillar, 9
cauliflower, 34
CD (compact disc), 4
ceiling, 29
celery, 34
cereal, 36
chair, 5
chairlift, 51
chalk, 28
changing room, 51
checkout, 35
cheek, 38
cheese, 32, 34

chef, 40
cherry, 33
chest (body), 38
chest of drawers, 5
chicken, 37
chicks, 24
children, 17
chimney, 12
chin, 38
chips, 37
chocolate, 32
chop, 42
chopsticks, 37
Christmas day, 47
Christmas tree, 47
cinema, 13
circle, 52
circus, 55
clean, 44
clementine, 33
cliff, 27
climb, 43
climbing, 51
clock, 6
closed, 44
clothes, 39
clouds, 48
clown, 55
coat, 39
cobweb, 11
cockerel, 24
coffee, 36
cold, 45
colours, 52
comb, 5
comic, 31
computer, 31
cone, 52
control tower, 21
cook, 43
cooker, 7
cotton wool, 30
country, 22
cousin, 41
cow, 25
cowshed, 25

crab, 26
crane, 15
crawl, 42
crayons, 29
cream, 36
crescent, 52
cricket (sport), 50
crisps, 33
crocodile, 18
crossing, 13
crutches, 30
cry, 42
cube, 52
cubs (fox), 23
cubs (lion), 18
cucumber, 34
cupboard, 7
cups, 7
curtain, 30
cushion, 4
cut, 42
cycling, 51

d

dance, 42, 50
dancers, 40
dark, 45
daughter, 41
days, 46, 47
dead, 45
deck chair, 27
deer, 19
dentist, 41
desk, 28
dew, 48
diamond, 52
dice, 14
difficult, 45
dig, 42
digger, 12
dinner, 36, 37
dirty, 44
diving, 50
doctor, 30, 31

dodgems, 54
dog, 16, 49, 55
doing things, 42
dolls, 14
doll's house, 14
dolphin, 18
donkey, 27
door, 6
door handle, 29
downstairs, 45
drawer, 7
drawing, 28
drawing pins, 28
dress, 39
dressing gown, 30
drill, 10, 12
drink, 42
drums, 14
dry, 44
duck, 17
ducklings, 17, 24
ducks, 24
dustbin, 8
duster, 7, 10
dustpan, 7
duvet, 5

e

eagle, 18
ears, 38
earth, 17
easel, 29
easy, 45
eat, 42
egg, 36
eggs, 35
eight, 53
eighteen, 53
elbow, 38
elephant, 19
eleven, 53
empty, 45
engine, 20
evening, 46
exercise, 50

eye, 38
eyebrow, 38

f

face, 38
face paints, 15
factory, 13
fairground, 54
fall, 43
families, 41
fancy dress, 33
far, 44
farm, 24
farmer, 25
farmhouse, 25
fast, 45
fat, 44
father, 41
Father Christmas, 47
feathers, 18
felt-tips, 28
fence, 25
few, 44
field, 25
fifteen, 53
fight, 43
file, 11
fingers, 38
fire engine, 13
fireman, 40
fireworks, 32
first, 44
fish, 27
fisherman, 23
fishing, 50
fishing boat, 27
fishing rod, 50
five, 53
flag, 26
flats, 13
flippers, 27
floor, 29
flour, 35
flower bed, 16
flowers, 8

fly, 11
fog, 48
food, 36, 49
foot, 58
football, 51
forest, 22
fork (garden), 9
forks, 6
four, 53
fourteen, 53
fox, 22
fox cubs, 23
Friday, 46
fridge, 6
fried egg, 36
frog, 16
frogman, 41
front, 45
frost, 48
fruit, 34
fruit juice, 33
frying pan, 7
full, 45

g

garage, 20
garden, 8
gate, 16
geese, 24
ghost train, 54
giraffe, 18
girl, 29
glasses (for drinking), 6
globe, 29
gloves, 39
glue, 28
goat, 19
goldfish, 49
good, 44
goods train, 20
gorilla, 18
grandfather, 41
grandmother, 41
grapefruit, 34
grapes, 31

grass, 8
green, 52
greenhouse, 9
grey, 52
guinea pig, 49
guitar, 14
gun, 15
gym, 50

h

hair, 38
hairdresser, 41
hall, 5
ham, 37
hamburger, 37
hammer, 11
hamster, 49
hand, 38
handbag, 35
handkerchief, 39
hang-gliding, 51
hard, 45
hat, 39
hay, 25
haystack, 24
head, 38
headlights, 20
hedge, 9
hedgehog, 22
helicopter, 21
helmet, 51
helter-skelter, 54
hen house, 24
hens, 25
hide, 43
high, 44
hill, 23
hippopotamus, 18
hoe, 8
hole, 12
holiday, 47
home, 4
honey, 36
hoop, 55
hoop-la, 54

horns, 19
horse, 25, 51
hosepipe, 9
hospital, 30
hot, 45
hot-air balloon, 22
hot chocolate, 36
hotel, 12
house, 13
husband, 41

i

iceberg, 18
ice cream, 16
ice skates, 51
ice-skating, 51
in, 45
iron, 7
ironing board, 6
island, 26

j

jacket, 39
jack-in-the-box, 33
jam, 36
jars, 11, 35
jeans, 39
jigsaw, 30
jogging, 51
judge, 40
judo, 51
juggler, 55
jump, 42
jumper, 39

k

kangaroo, 18
karate, 50
kennel, 49
kettle, 7
key, 6

kitchen, 6
kite, 16
kitten, 49
knee, 38
knit, 42
knives, 7

l

ladder, 9, 10
ladybird, 8
lake, 16
lambs, 24
lamp, 5, 29
lamp post, 13
last, 44
laugh, 42
lawn mower, 9
lead (dog), 17
leaves (one leaf), 9
leek, 34
left, 44
leg, 38
lemon, 34
leopard, 19
letters, 5
lettuce, 34
lift, 30
light, 45
lighthouse, 26
lightning, 48
lion, 19
lips, 38
listen, 42
living room, 4
lizard, 22
lock, 22
locker, 51
loft, 24
logs, 23
long, 45
lorry, 13
lorry driver, 41
low, 44
lunch, 36

m

make, 42
man, 12
many, 44
map, 29
marbles, 15
market, 13
mashed potatoes, 37
masks, 15
mat, 54
matches, 7
me, 38
meat, 35
mechanics, 40
medicine, 30
melon, 34
milk, 36, 49
mirror, 5
mist, 48
modelling dough, 15
mole, 23
Monday, 46
money, 35
money box, 15
monkey, 18
moon, 46
mop, 7
morning, 46
moth, 23
mother, 41
motor-boat, 26
motorcycle, 13
mountain, 23
mouse, 49
mouth, 38
mouth organ, 15
mud, 24
mushroom, 34
my, 39

n

nails, 10
nappy, 31

near, 44
neck, 38
necklace, 14
net, 27
new, 45
newspaper, 5
night, 46
nightdress, 31
nine, 53
nineteen, 53
nose, 38
notebook, 29
numbers, 53
nurse, 30
nuts, 11

o

oar, 26
oil, 21
oil tanker, 27
old, 45
omelette, 37
one, 53
onion, 34
open, 44
opposite words, 44
orange (colour), 52
orange (fruit), 31
orchard, 25
ostrich, 18
out, 45
oval, 52
over, 44
owl, 23

p

paddle, 27
paint, 42
painter, 41
paint pot, 11
paints, 15, 28
pancakes, 36
panda, 18

pants, 39
paper, 29
paper chain, 32
parachute, 15
park, 16
parrot, 49
party, 32
path, 9, 16
pavement, 12
paws, 18
peach, 34
pear, 31
peas, 34
pebbles, 27
pegs (for clothes), 5
pelican, 18
pen, 28
pencil, 28
penguin, 18
penknife, 10
people, 40
pepper, 36
petrol, 21
petrol pump, 21
petrol tanker, 21
pet, 41
pets, 49
photographer, 47
photographs, 28
piano, 15
pick, 43
picnic, 16
pictures, 5
pigeon, 8
piglets, 25
pigs, 25
pigsty, 24
pillow, 5
pills, 30
pilot, 21
pineapple, 35
pink, 52
pipes, 12
pizza, 37
plane (tool), 11
plane (vehicle), 21, 47
planet, 46

plank, 10
plant, 29
plaster, 30
plates, 7
platform, 20
play, 43
playground, 12
plough, 25
plum, 35
pockets, 39
polar bear, 19
pole, 55
police car, 12
policeman, 13, 40
policewoman, 40
pond, 24
pony, 51
popcorn, 54
postman, 41
potatoes, 35, 37
pram, 9
present, 47
presents, 33
pudding, 37
puddle, 17
pull, 43
pumpkin, 35
puppets, 15
puppy, 49
purple, 52
purse, 35
push, 43
push chair, 17
pyjamas, 31

r

rabbit, 49, 55
race, 50
racing car, 15
racket, 50
radiator, 5
radio, 4
railings, 17
railway station, 20

railway track, 20
rain, 48
rainbow, 48
rake, 9
raspberry, 33
read, 43
recorder, 14
rectangle, 52
red, 52
reindeer, 47
rhinoceros, 19
ribbon, 32
rice, 37
riding, 51
rifle range, 54
right, 44
ring, 14
ring master, 55
river, 22
road, 22
robot, 14
rocket, 15
rocking horse, 15
rocks, 22
roller, 13, 15
roller blades, 16
rolls (bread), 36
roof, 12
rope, 27
rope ladder, 55
roundabout, 54
rowing, 50
rowing boat, 27
rubber, 28
rubbish, 6
rug, 5
rugby, 50
ruler, 28
run, 43
runway, 21

s

saddle, 25
safety net, 55
sailing, 50

sailing boat, 26
sailor, 26
salad, 37
salami, 33
salt, 36
sandals, 39
sandcastle, 26
sandpaper, 10
sandpit, 16
sandwich, 32
Saturday, 46
sauce, 37
saucepans, 6
saucers, 7
sausage, 33
saw, 10
sawdust, 10
scales, 35
scarecrow, 25
scarf, 39
school, 12, 28
scissors, 28
screwdriver, 10
screws, 11
sea, 26
seagull, 26
seal, 19
seaside, 26
seasons, 48
seaweed, 27
seeds, 8
seesaw, 17
seven, 53
seventeen, 53
sew, 43
shapes, 52
shark, 19
shavings (wood), 10
shed, 8
sheep, 25
sheepdog, 24
sheet, 5
shell, 27
shepherdess, 25
ship, 27
shirt, 39

shoelace, 39
shoes, 39
shop, 12, 34
short, 45
shorts, 39
shoulders, 38
shower, 4
signals, 20
signpost, 22
sing, 43
singers, 40
sink, 7
sister, 41
sit, 43
six, 53
sixteen, 53
skateboard, 17
ski, 51
skiing, 51
ski pole, 51
skip, 43
skipping rope, 17
skirt, 39
sky, 48
sleep, 43
sleigh, 47
slide, 16
slippers, 31
slow, 45
small, 44
smile, 42
smoke, 9
snail, 8
snake, 19
snow, 48
snowboarding, 50
soap, 4
socks, 39
sofa, 4
soft, 45
soldiers, 15
son, 41
soup, 37
space, 46
spacemen, 15
spaceship, 46

spade, 8, 26
spaghetti, 37
spanner, 21
special days, 47
spider, 11
spinach, 35
sponge, 4
spoons, 7
sport, 50
spring, 48
sprinkler, 8
square, 52
squirrel, 22
stable, 25
stairs, 5
star, 46, 52
starfish, 26
steps, 13
sticking plaster, 31
sticks, 9
stones, 22
stool, 6
straw, 32
straw bales, 25
strawberry, 33
stream, 22
street, 12
string, 17
submarine, 14
sugar, 36
suitcase, 20
summer, 48
sumo wrestling, 51
sums, 28
sun, 46, 48
Sunday, 46
sunhat, 27
supper, 37
swans, 16
sweatshirt, 39
sweep, 43
sweet, 32
swimming, 50
swimming pool, 50
swimsuit, 27
swings, 16

switch, 6
syringe, 30

t

table, 5
tablecloth, 33
table tennis, 51
tacks, 11
tadpoles, 16
tail, 18
take, 43
talk, 42
tanker, 24
tanker (oil), 27
tanker (petrol), 21
tap, 4
tape measure, 11
target, 51
taxi, 13
tea, 36
teacher, 29
teapot, 36
teaspoons, 6
tea towel, 6
teddy bear, 31
teeth, 38
telephone, 5
telescope, 46
television, 31
ten, 53
tennis, 50
tents, 23
thermometer, 30
thin, 44
think, 42
thirteen, 53
three, 53
throw, 42
thumb, 38
Thursday, 46
ticket inspector, 20
ticket machine, 20
tie, 39
tiger, 19

tightrope, 55
tightrope walker, 55
tights, 39
tiles, 7
tins, 35
tissues, 31
toad, 23
toast, 36
toes, 38
toilet, 4
toilet paper, 4
tomato, 34
tongue, 38
tool box, 10
toothbrush, 4
toothpaste, 4
top, 44
top hat, 55
tortoise, 19
tourists, 47
towel, 4
toys, 31, 32
toyshop, 14
tractor, 24
traffic lights, 13
trailer, 13
train, 23
train driver, 20
trainers, 39
train set, 14
trapeze, 55
travel, 20
tray, 30
tree, 9
trees, 17
triangle, 52
trick cyclist, 55
tricycle, 17
trolley, 35
trousers, 39
trowel, 9
trumpet, 15
trunk, 19
T-shirt, 39
Tuesday, 46

tummy, 38
tunnel, 23
turkeys, 25
twelve, 53
twenty, 53
two, 53
tyre, 21

U

umbrella, 26, 48
uncle, 41
under, 44
upstairs, 45

V

vacuum cleaner, 6
van, 13
vegetables, 34
vest, 39
vet, 49
vice, 10
video, 5
video camera, 33
village, 23

W

wait, 43
waiter, 41
waiting room, 31
waitress, 41
walk, 43
walking stick, 31
wall, 29
wardrobe, 5
wash, 42
washbasin, 4
washing machine, 7
washing powder, 6
wasp, 8

wastepaper bin, 29
watch, 30, 43
water, 4
waterfall, 23
watering can, 8
water-skier, 26
waves, 27
weather, 48
wedding day, 47
Wednesday, 46
wet, 44
whale, 19
wheel, 20
wheelbarrow, 8
wheelchair, 30
whistle, 14
white, 52
wife, 41
wind, 48
windmill, 22
window, 32
windsurfing, 50
wing, 18
winter, 48
wolf, 18
woman, 13
wood, 11
workbench, 10
workshop, 10
worm, 8
write, 42

Y

yacht, 17
yellow, 52
yoghurt, 35

Z

zebra, 19
zip, 39
zoo, 18

This edition first published in 2002 by Usborne Publishing Ltd, Usborne House, 83-85 Saffron Hill, London EC1N 8RT.
www.usborne.com
Based on a previous title first published in 1979.